Whose Shoe?

by Eve Bunting

Illustrated by Sergio Ruzzier

CLARION BOOKS Houghton Mifflin Harcourt
Boston New York

Clarion Books
215 Park Avenue South
New York, New York 10003

Clarion Books is an imprint of Houghton Mifflin Harcourt
Publishing Company.

www.hmhco.com

The illustrations in this book were done in pen and ink
and watercolors on paper.
The text was set in Le Havre Rounded Light.

Library of Congress Cataloging-in-Publication Data
Bunting, Eve, 1928-
Whose shoe? / Eve Bunting ; illustrated by Sergio Ruzzier.
pages cm
Summary: A conscientious mouse tries to locate the owner of a
single unclaimed shoe.
ISBN 978-0-544-30210-5 (hardcover)
[1. Stories in rhyme. 2. Shoes—Fiction. 3. Lost and found
possessions—Fiction. 4. Mice—Fiction. 5. Animals—Fiction.]
I. Ruzzier, Sergio, illustrator. II. Title.
PZ8.3.B92We 2003
[E]—dc23
2014021787

Manufactured in China
SCP 10 9 8 7 6 5 4 3 2 1
4500519116

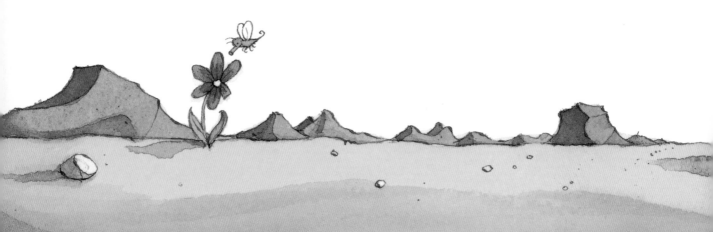

There's something in
that tall bamboo.

Oh, my goodness!
It's a shoe!

Finders keepers? That's not true.
I'll find the owner of this shoe.

"Tiger! I have found a shoe!
Who has lost it? Was it you?"

"It wasn't I. As you can see,
  that shoe would be too small for me.
  My feet are dainty, but I know
  my claws need space if they're to grow."

"But someone's lost it, don't you see?
For him that's a catastrophe.
He might still have the other shoe
and be unhappy. Wouldn't you?
I'll try to find him. I'll pursue it.
It will be good if I can do it."

"Spider, I have found a shoe.
I know it's way too big for you.
Still, I want to be polite —
I'm asking everyone in sight."

"I see your mother taught you well.
  You've got good manners, I can tell!

"My shoes are tiny. You are right.
I always tie the laces tight.
If I lost one, I'd be upset—
spider shoes are hard to get.
I have eight. I take great care
of all my shoes, since they are rare."

"Myna Bird, is this your shoe?
I think it might belong to you."

"That shoe would be too big for me.
As I fly high from tree to tree,
it might fall off on someone's head.
I leave my shoes at home instead.
It's very nice of you to try,
but shoes are useless if you fly."

"Hippo, have you lost this shoe?
I found it in the tall bamboo."

"There's one thing I find hard to take
when I'm standing in my lake:
I hate that mud between my toes.
(I'm rather fussy, I suppose.)
So I wear shoes. I have four pair,
and I don't really need a spare.

I want to thank you for inquiring.
Your honesty is quite inspiring."

"Hello! I've found a lonesome shoe.
Someone lost it. Was it you?"

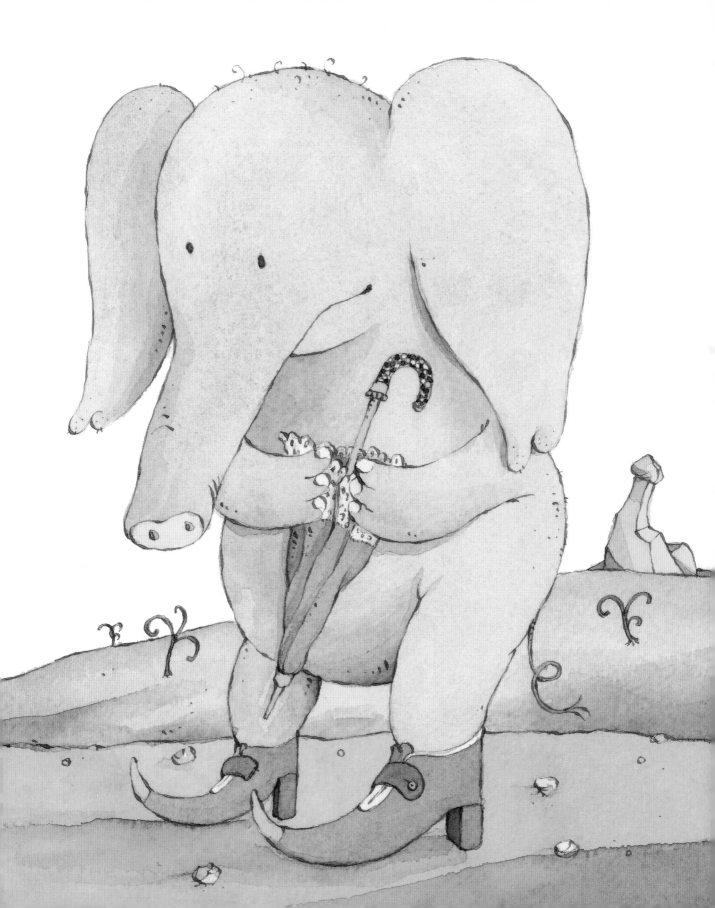

" I'd never wear a shoe like that.
    I like high heels, and that one's flat.
    These high heels make my ankles trim.
    They make my legs look really slim.
    So, thank you, but I must decline—
    my high-heeled shoes suit me just fine."

"Good morning to you, Kangaroo.
I found this handsome, lonesome shoe."

"Oh, goodness me! That is my shoe!
I threw it into the bamboo.

I have to say I am astounded
that you actually found it.
It hurt my foot. That made me cross.
I gave the shoe a hearty toss.

Would you like to have this shoe?
It's not worn out. It's still brand-new."

"Thank you kindly, Kangaroo.
    That's so considerate of you!
    I know exactly what to do
    with this handsome, lonesome shoe."

Who says that shoes are just for feet?
I'm glad my search is now complete.
The stars are shining overhead. . . .
I'm happy in my king-size bed!